**COULD SHE TRUST HIM . . .**
**OR WOULD HE BETRAY THEM ALL?**

When the three soldiers walked into the meeting in the forest a rush of fear swept through the small assembly. They had been discovered! This would be the end of their gatherings . . . possibly worse.

Tanya dared to approach the uniformed men. Their leader (he called himself Gregori) told her they were Christians! Had she finally found the friend who could make her dreams come true? Would Gregori bring her a Bible as he promised? Or would he betray the little girl who trusted him . . . and her frightened family who feared he was a spy . . .?

# TANYA
## and the
## Border Guard

**Anita Deyneka**

## David C. Cook Publishing Co.
850 NORTH GROVE AVENUE • ELGIN, IL 60120

In Canada: David C. Cook Publishing (Canada) Ltd., Weston, Ontario M9L 1T4

To my husband, Peter Deyneka, Jr.,
my source of ideas and inspiration

# Contents

# 1

# Footsteps
# in the Dungeon

The grim fortress loomed ahead. Its towering stone walls rose black and foreboding from the Neva River.

"Alexi, are you sure Momma won't mind if we stop at the fortress?" Tanya asked, stopping to tighten the strap on her canvas book bag.

"Of course it's all right, Tanya," Alexi shouted impatiently at his younger sister who lagged behind. "You know Momma and Poppa don't care if we're late getting home from school today. It's bad enough to go to school at all on Saturday."

"Maybe it's not getting home on time that you're so worried about," Alexi teased. "Could it be that big, cold, black dungeon that scares you?" He waved Tanya on toward Peter and Paul Fortress Island, home of the old dungeon.

Challenged, Tanya made a dash to catch up with her brother. Her long black braids swished wildly against her blue canvas coat.

Alexi led Tanya across Nevsky Prospekt, Leningrad's wide, busy street near the Moika Canal. As soon as they reached the water's edge, Alexi picked up a stone and hurled it across the canal's silky water. Tanya shifted her heavy book bag again as she watched the stones skip across the water.

As long as she had lived in Leningrad, a city of islands laced together by lazy canals, she was always eager to lean over the canal stone walls and watch the water move silently by.

Sometimes she pretended she saw Russian traders bundled in heavy fur coats steering their boats loaded with treasures. She dreamed of 300 years ago when these ancient waterways were first built as Leningrad's main roads.

Letting her imagination flow with the water, Tanya tried to feel what it might have been like to be a slave of the strong czar king, Peter the Great, who built this city on acres of soggy swampland. She had read about 200,000 Russians who died building these canals. The city was called St. Petersburg then.

Only a few weeks ago Tanya's teacher had explained: "The huge fortress that Peter the Great constructed became more than just a fortress. It was on an island and difficult to

escape. The czars of Russia used it as a dungeon —a prison for their most dangerous criminals."

Alexi hurled the last pebble across the canal. He grabbed his book bag and jogged across the bridge toward the Peter and Paul Fortress Island.

He slowed at the entrance to the island museum just long enough for Tanya to catch up. The bored guard leaning against the wide entrance gate glanced dutifully at the two of them and with a nod motioned them inside the fortress.

Inside Alexi dashed ahead again. "Let's run down to the water first," he shouted. Tanya was breathless and red-cheeked from trying to keep up. "Then we'll tour the old dungeon."

Tanya scanned the island. She admired the old, gold-domed churches. She twisted to see the tops of the high church spires reaching to the clouds. She and Alexi raced along the craggy stone walls originally built to turn back invaders.

Once inside the mammoth dungeon, Tanya felt warmer. But she didn't feel braver. "I-I'm not sure I want to go through the dungeon," she objected. "There's nobody else here and the last time we went through with Momma and Poppa —well, I was sort of scared, Alexi."

Alexi shoved his black hair from his eyes. "Come on, Tanya—you wouldn't want me to leave you here alone, would you?" With a teasing grin to encourage his timid sister, he sprinted boldly ahead.

A cold dreary mist from the river soaked into every crevice of the long, half-lighted halls that wound through the dungeon.

Tanya hung back. Were the walls as slimy as they looked? While she cautiously touched their clammy stones, she didn't notice Alexi's silhouette fade into the shadows of the hall ahead.

Suddenly she realized she was alone in the eerie hall. She glanced around. Nobody in sight! "Alexi, wait for me!" she shouted. The deserted hall echoed her frightened call.

She turned and ran. If she could only catch up with Alexi—but her book bag kept slipping. She stopped and jerked the shoulder strap tight. She looked ahead for Alexi. But his lithe, dark figure was swallowed in the cavernous tunnel.

She ran with long, healthy strides. No Alexi. Alarmed, she ran faster but Alexi was hidden in the black distance beyond her.

Tanya had been sure that she and Alexi were alone. She was sure no one else had come into the dungeon.

But as she ran, footsteps seemed to close in on her from behind. They pounded louder. She was too scared to look back.

She listened.

Desperately she wished she could hear her brother's familiar steps ahead. But the steps were not Alexi's—they were quick, small, hurrying steps. And they were rapidly catching her. Tanya panicked. The faster she ran to escape the steps, the closer they came.

"I shouldn't have let Alexi talk me into exploring this creepy, old place," she thought. Pictures of criminals who once occupied the dungeon's musty cells came into her mind. She imagined a cold hand reaching out to clutch her shoulder, and she shuddered.

Her frightened thoughts tumbled. She clung to the heavy book bag and ran harder.

Finally in the semidarkness ahead she saw Alexi stooping to tie his shoe. "Alexi, wait!" she screamed.

When she reached her brother she felt safe. She was also breathless, frightened, and half angry. "Alexi, how could you run off and leave me alone? Somebody was chasing me," she panted.

"Chasing you?" Alexi's questioning brown eyes glanced past his sister's shoulder to see if someone might be there.

"Yes, chasing me. I'm positive. When I started to run, I heard footsteps. And they kept coming closer and closer."

"So they kept coming closer and closer," Alexi said deliberately as if he were seriously trying to unravel her story. Then he grinned. "When you finally caught up with me—think hard—then what happened to the steps?"

"I—I'm not sure," Tanya hesitated.

"My brave, bold sister," Alexi laughed, "the dangerous footsteps which chased you were nothing more than the sound of your own steps. You know how everything echoes in this old dungeon."

"Yow!" he yelled.

"Yow . . . yow . . . yow" his voice reverberated through the hollow dungeon. "See what I mean?"

Embarrassed, Tanya saw exactly what Alexi meant. "Anyway, you shouldn't have deserted me and I don't want to stay any longer in this creepy old place," she said firmly.

Still laughing, Alexi led the way out of the dungeon. "Wow, you were really jumpy—you were acting just like a girl!"

"Maybe you'd be jumpy too after what happened at school today," Tanya said. She was glad to be outside the gloomy dungeon. She warmed herself in the sun which had struggled out from behind the clouds.

Alexi found a stone and slung it past the wall far out into the sea. "Did your teacher say something about Christians again today?" Alexi asked, his dark eyes suddenly sober.

"Well, it wasn't exactly about being a Christian," Tanya explained. "But I think that's what she really meant." Tanya slid her heavy book bag to the ground. "Meria Petrovna lectured me about not wearing the red scarf—in front of the whole class," Tanya's voice quavered.

"What would you have done, Alexi? Meria Petrovna knows I won't wear the scarf because I am a Christian. I already explained to her why I can't join the Young Communist Pioneer Club and wear the red scarf. Just like Momma and Poppa said, I told her I couldn't join a club that was against God because I am a Christian. I

15

can't deny God just to be a member of the Pioneers, can I?" Tanya's voice shook indignantly.

"Tanya," Alexi cautioned, "don't talk so loud. You know what Poppa said about being more careful. What if somebody's listening?"

Tanya tossed her black braids over her shoulder. "Nobody is listening. How could anyone hear us out here? Anyway, why should we always have to be quiet?" Tanya pouted. "I don't care who's listening. Meria Petrovna didn't care who was listening today when she made me stand in front of the whole class." Tears began to well up in Tanya's eyes. "Alexi, don't you see? Pretty soon everybody in class is going to be afraid to talk to me. I won't have any friends when we go to school camp this summer."

"Come on, Tanya. Don't imagine new problems," Alexi chided. He grabbed her heavy book bag and Tanya knew it was his way of saying he felt sorry. He tried to take Tanya's mind from her troubles. "Besides, aren't we supposed to put the borscht on the stove before Momma comes home from work? We'd better hurry!"

Inside their small three-room apartment on the fifth floor of the Zadgordski apartment building, Tanya smelled vegetables cooking in the borscht and knew her mother was already home. The apartment was warm and the table set. Mrs. Markarovitch turned from the small stove, gathered both of the children into her arms, and welcomed them with a hug.

In a few minutes the apartment door swung wide as a strong man with merry eyes and a very black mustache entered and kissed his wife.

"Poppa!" Tanya cried, hugging her father.

"Tanyatchka." Tanya smiled. She liked to hear her father call her by her nickname.

"Ivan, you are late, but praise God you are still on time for the broadcast," Mrs. Makarovitch said while she poured the thick soup into the bowls and arranged them on the table. "We will have to eat while we listen."

"Alexi, cut the bread. Tanya, put the sour cream on the table for the borscht." Mrs. Makarovitch stood in the tiny kitchen stirring the soup. The warmth from the kitchen made her blond curls straggle across her forehead. Mrs. Makarovitch briskly pushed them back.

"Our adventurous children were also late," Mrs. Makarovitch explained to her husband, pretending to frown. "They were on an exploring expedition to the Peter and Paul Fortress."

The bowls of red, creamy borscht steamed on the table. Mr. Makarovitch tuned in the radio to the Christian broadcast.

"You are listening to the Russian Gospel broadcast from Quito, Ecuador, the Voice of the Andes," the missionary announcer said clearly.

Mr. Makarovitch smiled. "Tonight the signal is clear. Praise God there is no static. It is a miracle."

"I think radio is a miracle God invented especially for Russia, Poppa," Alexi whispered importantly.

After the broadcast, Tanya hunched over the wooden table for a long time writing notes into a little leather book.

"Tanya," her father smiled, "How many girls your age would copy Bible verses every night from the radio broadcasts as faithfully as you do? Tanyatchka," he continued solemnly, "I don't want to discourage you. However, since you've never held a Bible in your hands, you do not realize that it is a big book. It is actually many books in one. Don't be disappointed if your copied Bible grows slowly. It will take a long time."

Thoughtfully, Tanya laid her notebook on the table. "But, Poppa, if we could only buy a Bible. Our government prints other books—why won't they print Bibles? And when there are so many Christians just like us who want one so much. It's just not fair!"

"Tanya," Alexi said smugly, "Momma and Poppa shouldn't have to keep explaining to you. You know we're different from other people."

Tanya sulked. "Just because you're older, it doesn't mean you know everything."

"Children," Mrs. Makarovitch interrupted. "Such arguing, and just after we heard the radio preacher say we should give thanks in everything."

Mrs. Makarovitch put an arm around her daughter to console her. "Tanyatchka, think how much we have to thank the Lord for. Poppa has a good job as an engineer. Both Poppa and I have been allowed to keep our jobs even though the officials know we are Christians. We have a warm place to live. You and Alexi are receiving a free education like other Soviet citizens.

"And besides all this we have the Christian radio broadcasts coming to us from other countries. Thank God for that. We are not alone," Mrs. Makarovitch said gratefully. "Every day we can invite the radio missionaries right into our home. Every day we can hear the radio Bible."

"Of course I'm grateful, Momma," Tanya said grudgingly, "but it's just that I don't see why . . ."

Mr. Makarovitch gently interrupted his daughter, "Tanya, we will discuss this more later, but right now I think it is more important for you to hear my news. I have a surprise that even your mother doesn't know about." He winked at his wife across the table.

"Let me guess," Tanya volunteered. Her brown eyes twinkled with excitement. "I think . . . I think we are going to visit Baba in Czechoslovakia."

"No, Tanyatchka, we are not going to visit Grandma. At least not now. But we are going to see some good friends. Do you remember last fall when we went to the Christian meeting in Dobrovno Forest? Tomorrow afternoon the same Christians are gathering again and they have invited us to come."

"The woods! A meeting in the woods!" Alexi bounced from his chair. "We are going to go, aren't we, Poppa?"

"What about you, Tanyatchka?" Mr. Makarovitch asked. "Do you think you can walk that far? It's six miles, you know."

"Of course, Poppa, you know I can—just as well as Alexi. And I want to go. Her eyes gleamed. "Will Natasha be at the meeting? I haven't seen her for so long!"

Suddenly Tanya giggled, "Maybe Sonya Durasoff will be at the meeting. I think Alexi would walk six miles without even getting tired if he knew Sonya was going to be there!"

Alexi flushed. His freckles which were usually faded flamed across his nose. He tried to ignore his teasing sister.

Mrs. Makarovitch laughed. "Well, anyway, I'm sure there will be some Christian young people at the meeting and I think you'll both be glad to see them."

Everyone talked at once about the next day's expedition to Dobrovno. "We'll need a lunch," Mrs. Makarovitch remembered and took out the basket she used for shopping. She layered the bottom with brown wrapping paper and put a loaf of dark bread and a long sausage in it.

Tanya waited until everyone was in bed and she heard her father's steady snore coming from the bedroom. Then she crept from her own couch bed across the room to the bench where Alexi was sleeping.

"Alexi! Alexi! Are you sleeping yet?" Alexi only mumbled drowsily in reply. She shook his arm. "Listen, I have something important to tell you!" Alexi rubbed his eyes and sat up.

Quietly, so their parents couldn't hear, Tanya whispered, "Alexi, do you remember what I told you about Poppa's Bible?"

"You mean the Bible you wish Poppa had?" Alexi yawned. "Tanya, it's a good idea. But it's true what Poppa said—even though he doesn't know you are doing it for him. It will take you years to copy down the whole Bible from the radio. You just don't understand."

"Of course I understand," Tanya said firmly. "Maybe you don't understand," she whispered mysteriously. "I have a plan. I've been praying for a long time. I asked the Lord to show me how to find a Bible for Poppa. There will be hundreds of Christians at the meeting. Somebody at the meeting will know where I can find a Bible," she said confidently.

Alexi sat up wide awake. "That's impossible, Tanya. Most of the Christians at the meetings don't even have Bibles. You'll never find an extra one for Poppa!"

"Yes, I will," Tanya said with assurance. "I have a plan."

# 2

# Strangers
# Visit the Forest

Tanya snuggled against her father on the narrow seat. "Why does this bus have to stop so often," she wondered aloud. The canals reflected the misty, morning sunlight through the streaked windows of the lumbering bus.

"We still have so far to walk after we get off this slow old bus. I hope we won't be late for the meeting. I'll never find Natasha."

"Patience, Tanyatchka," Mr. Makarovitch said. "We still have a long way until the end of the bus line. Enjoy your ride. When we start walking you will wish you were still on this 'slow old bus,'" he chuckled.

On the outskirts of Leningrad, the woman

driver jerked the bus to its last stop. "Konetz!" she yelled. "Hurray!" Alexi shouted. "The end of the line!" He leaped out the back door.

Mr. Makarovitch handed the woman driver the ten kopecks to pay the bus fare for the venturesome family.

Beyond the paved road that marked the end of the bus route, Mr. Makarovitch turned onto a broad dirt trail. Alexi darted ahead on short exploration trips into the inviting forest. Tanya walked silently with her mother. She concentrated on her plan to find a Bible at the meeting.

"No rain—not even much fog. We can thank the Lord for giving us such a bright day for the meeting," Mrs. Makarovitch said. "And for our six-mile walk to the meeting," Mr. Makarovitch added. "I'm glad the white nights have started. We'll need the light for the walk home." Mr. Makarovitch was referring to Leningrad's summer days when some northern parts of Russia have nineteen hours of daylight.

"Poppa, are we going to follow this path all the way? The meeting is going to be in the clearing outside the Initsky Collective, isn't it?" Alexi called back.

"Yes, Alexi, you lead the way."

After two hours, the family stopped on the path to rest. "Soon we will meet some of the other Christians," Mr. Makarovitch cautioned. "But remember, we must not gather in a large group as we walk. It is best if the authorities do not know that so many of us are going to the Christian meeting." The sound of his voice trailed off into the majestic birch trees which stood like soldiers guarding the forest trail.

"Poppa," Alexi questioned seriously, "do you think our government will ever give Christians permission to meet freely?"

Mr. Makarovitch slowed his steady steps. "That is an answer that only the Lord knows. For now we must be grateful our government allows us to have at least one church open in Leningrad. We can meet on Sunday and sometimes once or twice during the week."

"Only one church," Tanya grumbled. "It's just not fair, Poppa. There are so many Christians in Leningrad. You said yourself that all the Christians couldn't fit into one church."

Mr. Makarovitch thought for several minutes before he answered. "It's true. One church is not enough for a city the size of Leningrad. That is why some groups of Christians meet in the woods. They have asked permission to meet in a building, but the government won't permit them.

"The Christians don't harm anyone and the government knows this, but still our government is atheistic—it is against Christians," Tanya's father said with a deep sigh.

"So we must remember," he warned, "even though our constitution says that Soviet citizens have the right to worship freely, the police still might stop our meeting in the woods. Or they could make us all pay a fine. It is even possible they might put some of our leaders in jail."

"And," Mrs. Makarovitch emphasized, "that

is why it so important that we ask God for His protection when we go to a meeting in the woods. It is the Lord we worship, and only He can protect us."

Mr. Makarovitch glanced at his watch and turned to his wife. "All this serious talk has made me hungry. It is already noon. Do you suppose we could make a picnic table on a stump and spread out our 'huge' lunch?" He hoisted the basket in mockery as if it were very heavy. A plump robin waddled across the path. He perked his head as if he had heard someone mention "lunch."

Half an hour later the Makarovitches had eaten their lunch of sausage, thick slices of black bread, and tomatoes, and were once again on the forest trail. The family trudged along single file—Alexi in front.

They passed several people on the forest path. Some carried picnic baskets. Others picked wild trilliums and violets which were blooming in scarce patches along the forest path. Some people traipsed off into the forest to hunt for mushrooms.

Tanya was glad when they at last met some other Christians. The women kissed one another and so did the men—three times in customary Russian fashion. An old babushka in a black dress bent to kiss Tanya. "Ah, little daughter," she smiled, "I wish my old legs were as nimble as yours."

By two o'clock they reached the meeting place. The woods, which had been thick with fir and pine trees huddled against tall birches, now began to thin out. A grassy meadow unfolded before them.

Tanya saw groups of people clustered like bushes around the sunny clearing. Most of them carried coats for the long walk home when the May night would turn cool. Others sat on logs and talked quietly.

Tanya spotted the group of teenagers first. "Over there—there they are," Tanya gestured. "Alexi," she whispered with a giggle, "guess what. Sonya Durasoff is there." Alexi shrugged indifferently and sauntered toward the group of teenagers.

Tanya spied Natasha. She was sitting on a log watching a group of adults practicing choir music. Her long, blond hair was swathed gracefully back with a fluffy blue scarf. "Natasha!" Tanya hugged her friend.

Tanya and Natasha chatted above the choir music floating through the forest. A gray whiskered squirrel played fearlessly close to their feet.

Tanya's brown eyes flashed with questions. "Natasha, who is your teacher? What is she like?"

Just as Tanya was about to tell Natasha all about her teacher, Meria Petrovna, Pastor Darmansky's voice boomed out over the meadow. "Brothers and sisters, it is time to begin."

The men separated to one side—the women to the other. Pastor Darmansky and five other pastors stood at the front. Everyone understood that the few logs scattered around the clearing were only for the babushkas and dedjas (grandmothers and grandfathers) to sit on.

"First we shall begin with prayer," Pastor Darmansky's powerful voice resounded over the congregation of 300 people.

Tanya and her mother stood near the back of the crowd. Tanya studied the rows of women in front of her. All the women and some of the girls wore colorful scarves—in Russia a symbol of worship to God. Tanya was glad her mother reminded her to wear her blue scarf. She fingered the knot tied severely under her chin.

The Christians knelt all across the meadow. Many prayed softly. Pastor Darmansky's voice rose above the others. "We praise You, God, the Father of Heaven and earth, that we could meet here to worship You in this beautiful forest cathedral. We are thankful that we are Your children. Help us to be faithful to You . . . in our jobs . . . in school . . ."

Tanya's toes stirred. She moved closer to her mother, who was whispering softly, "Da Gospodee—Yes, Lord, yes, Lord."

Tanya closed her eyes tightly. "Prayer is the time to bring our praise and our problems to God," her father had often told her. "Please, Lord," she prayed earnestly, "Help me somehow to find a Bible today among all the Christians."

The pastor concluded his long prayer with an "amen." Then people all across the huge clearing took turns praying aloud. One woman

28

prayed for her husband who had lost his job because he was a believer. One man almost groaned as he prayed. He did not mention the problem, but Tanya could hear the suffering in his voice. "Come quickly, Lord Jesus," he pleaded.

The congregation sang one song after another and all from memory. A few people had laboriously copied by hand some of the songs from the radio broadcasts. But hymnbooks were as scarce as Bibles. Even the pastor knew the songs by heart—some he had written himself. The worshipful music filled the forest.

Tanya sang too, but her mind wandered to her plan. She had been praying for a long time, and hadn't the radio pastor said, "Everything is possible with God"? She thought about God and His Book. Somehow at this meeting with so many Christians, there would be some way. Somebody must have an extra Bible or know where she could buy one.

"Even if we have to pay a lot of money for it," Tanya's thoughts settled on her problem. "I know Poppa says they are very expensive, but somehow Momma and Poppa could save enough money. She knew that money was scarce at home. But she knew that her parents kept a little box under the bed where they put tithe money for church. There was another jar in the kitchen in which they saved money for special projects —like when they bought a new shortwave radio last Christmas.

Even as Tanya's plans increased, her hopes

fell. She surveyed the congregation in the forest. When Pastor Darmansky carefully opened his worn, black Bible, Tanya watched to see who else took out Bibles. She turned in so many different directions that her mother glanced disapprovingly.

But as far as she looked, Tanya could count only four people with real Bibles beside the one Pastor Darmansky held. Tanya watched a man with white hair and mustache stoop to follow the reading in his worn Bible. The people standing beside him strained to see the precious words.

Many of the people had little notebooks. Tanya guessed that most of the notebooks were Bible verses which they had copied from the Gospel radio broadcasts. "Only they've been copying theirs longer than I've been copying mine," she thought ruefully.

Abruptly Tanya realized she wasn't listening to the pastor read from the Bible. She had been too absorbed in her own plans. Now she watched Pastor Darmansky and concentrated closely —she didn't want to miss a single word from the Holy Book of God.

Except for the pastor's sonorous voice, the forest clearing was silent. A boy standing near Alexi shifted his foot and snapped a dry branch. The sharp noise crackled through the quiet congregation.

Pastor Darmansky read for almost an hour. Then Pastor Miroff preached.

Tanya thought she heard a strange cracking

in the distance. Distracted, she wondered if someone had stepped carelessly on dry wood again. Or maybe a forest animal had strayed into the meeting place.

But the crunching sounds grew steadily louder. Tanya listened intently. She recognized the sound. Steps! Her heart pounded.

The meeting had already been going on for two hours. Suspicious thoughts tightened Tanya's body with fear. "None of the Christians would be coming this late," she thought. Tanya saw her mother's attentive expression turn apprehensive.

Now there was no question. The steps came closer. Tanya turned and stared into the thick woods.

She knew Pastor Miroff must have heard the steps, but he continued preaching calmly. "Brothers and sisters, Jesus said, 'If they have persecuted me, they will also persecute you.' "

Tanya was terrified. Who could be coming? Was it the police? Her terror mounted as she remembered her father's grave words that morning on the trail. What if the police arrested some of the Christians? What if they made them pay fines or put them in jail? What if they arrested her father? She wanted to run to him now, throw her arms around his neck, and feel safe. But there was no place to run.

She huddled closer to her mother who stood stiff and silent. Mrs. Makarovitch shielded Tanya's shivering shoulder with her warm arm.

Tanya felt fear grip her like invisible strangling fingers. "But I have to know who's coming!" Furtively she glanced in the direction of the steps.

Through the trees she saw the men—three of them. Soon she clearly saw their tan uniforms . . . the badges . . . and the red stars. "Oh, Momma," she gasped, "they're soldiers!"

# 3

# The Secret Plan

"Soldiers, Momma, they're soldiers!" Tanya was so frightened she forgot to whisper. Mrs. Makarovitch never took her eyes off Pastor Miroff. She gazed resolutely ahead, but she circled Tanya's shoulders protectively.

Tanya was glad for her mother's reassuring arm, but it was almost impossible to stand still. She wanted to turn again and look at the soldiers.

Maybe she had made a mistake. Were they really soldiers? But they must be. She was certain the three men were wearing army uniforms.

Often she had seen soldiers on the streets of Leningrad wearing those same tan uniforms.

She thought of the May Day parade a few weeks ago. School was dismissed for the day. All the students in Leningrad lined up along Nevsky Boulevard and cheered the marching soldiers and huge tanks. Tanya remembered the hundreds of soldiers who had covered the boulevard like a huge blanket.

There was no doubt about it. The three men she had glimpsed in the forest were soldiers.

Tanya tried to be as brave as her mother. She fixed her eyes on Pastor Miroff, but her thoughts wavered. What were the other Christians thinking? Her mother's arm tightened about her shoulder. Tanya felt comforted, but she felt her mother's arm tremble.

The soldiers had stopped at the back of the crowd. Tanya tensed. Were they writing down names of Christians who were at the meeting? She remembered that the government especially disapproved of young people attending Christian meetings and she shivered.

Tanya listened anxiously for the sound of footsteps. Would the soldiers watch at the back or would they come to the front of the meeting? Would they order Pastor Miroff to stop preaching? Would they make arrests?

Tanya remembered once when she had been at a meeting in the church in Leningrad. She had overheard three Christian men talking about a meeting in the forest.

The men said that soldiers had come to the forest and had written down the names of many of the Christians. Then the soldiers had threatened the frightened Christians, "Either you pay the fine of 200 rubles for illegal assembly or we will take your pastor before the judge."

Nobody had that much money. But an enterprising young Christian man had taken a picnic basket and passed it among the believers. Soon there were 200 rubles—enough to pay the fine. The pastor was saved from the police.

Tanya felt deep into the pocket of her canvas coat. She had tied 25 kopecks in her handkerchief. She had been saving them for six months to buy a pair of skates.

Tanya could not resist taking one more glance. The three men were standing at the back of the meeting listening attentively to Pastor Miroff.

But Tanya was not reassured. "Maybe they are just waiting until the meeting is over to arrest us," she worried.

Pastor Miroff's steady voice broke into Tanya's thoughts, "Brothers and sisters, our Savior, Jesus, has said, 'Lo I am with you always, even unto the end of the world.' If we are believers, the Son of God lives in us. He is with us at this very moment. We have only to speak to Him in prayer."

And then after Pastor Miroff read once more from the Bible, the choir sang. One last prayer, and the meeting was over.

Usually after the Christian meetings the woods were filled with happy conversation. There were long good-byes. Friends embraced and prayed together. They knew they might not see one another for several months.

But today silence hung heavy in the spring air. A gloomy black cloud of fear had settled over the meadow. People moved hesitantly and talked in whispers. Everyone knew about the soldiers. Everyone wondered why they had come. Tanya's mother glanced apprehensively in the direction of the soldiers. Abruptly she whispered, "Tanya, hurry! Let's walk over to Poppa and Alexi."

Tanya and her mother weaved their way through the tight crowd. Tanya's mother stopped to embrace a friend, "Yekaterina Sergeyevna —it has been so many weeks since I've seen you. Yes, we must pray." Tanya's mother agreed soberly with Yekaterina Sergeyevna.

Tanya saw Alexi. "But, Momma," she cried, "where—where is Poppa? He is not with Alexi! Oh, Momma," Tanya's voice was stunned. "Do you see him? I don't see him anywhere!"

Quickly, Tanya and her mother reached Alexi who stood alone. Dazed, he stared off to the other side of the clearing.

"Alexi, where is Poppa?" Tanya cried. Alexi pointed in the direction of the three soldiers. "Poppa told me to wait and pray. He said he was going over to greet the three soldiers."

"But why did he go, Momma?" Tanya protested. "Oh, Momma, what will they do?"

Mrs. Makarovitch's ruddy cheeks were pinched and pale but she forced a smile. "Tanya, someone must greet the soldiers. We must trust the Lord to protect Poppa. And we

37

must also be very proud of him. Your father, you know, is a very brave man."

Tanya was proud of her father. In fact she was sure that there was no other man so brave and wonderful in all of Leningrad. She climbed up on a log, determined to see what would happen as her father neared the three soldiers.

The three intruders stood awkwardly by themselves. Tanya raised herself on tiptoes straining to see. Her father held out a friendly hand to one of the soldiers. Tanya held her breath. But to her astonishment, the soldier seemed to eagerly return her father's greeting.

In a few minutes, Tanya heard her father's familiar voice echo through the forest, "Brothers and sisters—may I please have your attention? Please return to your places. Our three friends here have an announcement they would like to make."

Tanya relaxed a little when she heard the word "friends." But what could it mean? Could soldiers be friends? "Please, Momma," she begged, "let's hurry. Let's stand near the front so we can hear the announcement."

The three soldiers and Tanya's father walked to the front of the clearing.

The tallest soldier stepped forward. "I wish to speak to all of you," he said almost shyly.

"He doesn't look angry, does he?" Alexi sounded relieved.

Impatiently Tanya shoved forward. "I can't see over the heads of the people."

"Quiet, Tanya. You can hear! Listen," her

mother said.

The tallest soldier continued pleasantly, "I regret very much that the appearance of soldiers at your meeting has frightened some of you. I should have realized that you would think we were here to bring you trouble. But it is not so. Please, you are our brothers and sisters. You see, I am a believer . . ."

An amazed gasp rippled through the crowd. Tanya heard whispers of "Slava Bogu—Praise God." People pushed forward, anxious not to miss a single word from the soldier.

The tall soldier introduced himself, "I am Gregori Alexandrovich. These are my friends, Andrey Dmitrich and Nikolai Fydorovich." With a smile the tall soldier motioned to the other two soldiers. "You see, my two friends are also believers."

Again grateful cries of "Slava Bogu—Praise God" rose from the crowd. Pastor Prokoff was so excited that he walked up to the three soldiers and hugged each one of them. "Brothers," he beamed, "you must tell us how this wonderful event happened to you. Tell us so that we can praise God with you."

Andrey Dmitrich, the youngest of the three soldiers, smiled at the tall soldier. "You became a believer first, Gregori. Maybe you should tell the story."

Gregori rested his large foot on a log and said, "At the army base my friends and I began to listen to the Christian broadcasts from Monaco. I believed in Jesus and then I invited my two friends, Andrey and Nikolai, to listen to the broadcasts on my radio. They also believed."

A warm spring wind from the forest ruffled Gregori's heavy army coat. He took it off and folded it carefully across his arm and continued his story. "There is an old lady in the army kitchen who is a Christian. All the soldiers in our unit ridicule her.

"But when Nikolai, Andrey, and I became Christians ourselves, we secretly went to see her. We asked her if she knew where we could find a Bible. She didn't have a Bible herself and didn't have any to give us. But she did give us some good advice." Gregori smiled. "She knew about your meetings in the woods. She told us if we came here, someone would have a Bible and we could hear God's Word."

"So you see," Gregori concluded, "that is how we happened to come to your meeting. But please," he pleaded, "don't be frightened. Please believe that we three also know the forgiveness of God. We only want to worship God with you."

As soon as Gregori finished speaking, a few of the Christians hung back suspiciously. But most of the believers surrounded the three soldiers. They hugged them, shook their hands, and asked them questions. Tanya and Alexi were caught in the crowd and were carried along toward the front.

They overheard excited conversation: "Weren't you afraid to come here to our meeting? Is it not difficult to serve Christ while you are in the army?"

Tanya and Alexi hung timidly at the edge of the excited crowd encircling the soldiers—just close enough to hear.

Suddenly Tanya clutched Alexi's sleeve, "Quick, Alexi, follow me over here where we can talk. Hurry, I have an idea." She tugged at her reluctant brother.

Alexi protested with a bewildered frown, "We'll lose our places. I want to hear what the soldiers say." But Tanya was so insistent that he finally followed his sister.

"Sh-sh," Tanya's fingers flew impulsively to her lips and she began to whisper. "Listen, Alexi, I have a secret!"

"A secret," Alexi echoed with an exasperated shrug. "I'm going back to the soldiers. Tanya, why do you always have to pretend everything is so mysterious? You can tell me your secret later. I don't want to miss the soldiers."

"Alexi! Listen." Tanya's brown eyes pleaded. "You've got to help me. I want to talk to the soldiers. Somehow I've got to talk to them." Then she bluntly confided her plan, "I'm going to ask them if they can help me find a Bible for Poppa!"

"You're going up and talk to a soldier by yourself?" Alexi whispered indignantly. "You're afraid of spiders and mice and everything else. And you're going to go talk to a soldier?" he asked incredulously. "Besides," he hissed sternly, "what will Momma and Poppa say if we talk to the soldiers by ourselves—especially if

41

we ask them to help us find a Bible? Anyway, those soldiers don't have Bibles. You heard them say so yourself. They're looking for Bibles, too."

"But that's just it," Tanya interrupted happily. "They're looking for Bibles. Only they have a chance of finding them. They're soldiers. I remember Poppa said Anatoli Alexandrovich bought a Bible from a soldier who was a border guard.

"At least we should try, Alexi. They're soldiers and they will have some idea of what we should do. Please, Alexi," she begged, "we've got to find a way to talk to those soldiers."

Alexi frowned. He burrowed his fists deep into his pockets.

"It's impossible," he said finally. "How would you pay the soldiers for a Bible even if they could find one? And besides," Alexi dropped his voice mysteriously, "what if they are spies?"

"Spies!" Tanya's eyes opened wide.

"Yes, spies," Alexi whispered. He glanced furtively to see if anyone was listening. "I remember my friend Yuri told me about a policeman who came to his church. The policeman told the Christians he was a believer. He even said he wanted to be baptized," Alexi said scornfully. "But the policeman was really a government spy. He told lies about the Christians and tried to get them in trouble with the government."

Alexi saw that Tanya was scared. He was sure that he had convinced his impetuous sister.

# 4

# Tanya
# Takes a Stand

Tanya didn't argue with Alexi as she usually would have. She knew he was telling the truth. There was a chance the soldiers might be informers.

But then she thought of Gregori and his sincere words, "Don't be afraid of us, we just want to worship God with you." She remembered how earnestly he had spoken.

Tanya made her decision—she would trust the soldiers. Because she trusted them she was determined. "I am going to try to talk to them. I believe them. I think the soldiers are Christians. Please," she tugged at her brother's sleeve, "please, Alexi, you've got to come with

43

me. I'm afraid to go to them alone."

"I should tell Momma and Poppa," he threatened, but instead he reluctantly walked after her. "I'm not going to talk to the soldiers for you," he warned.

By now the crowd had scattered and Tanya and Alexi walked straight to the soldier, Gregori. Boldly, Tanya stepped forward.

"Excuse me, comrade soldier . . ." Afraid to look straight at the soldier, Tanya fixed her eyes on the red stars on his uniform. "Could I talk to you—please?"

"Yes, little sister. Are you, too, a believer?"

The soldier's voice was so kind that Tanya gained the courage to look at him. His eyes were gentle and smiling too.

"Oh, yes—yes, I am a believer," she replied. She turned to Alexi who stood warily at her side. "Comrade soldier, this is my brother, Alexi Makarovitch." Gregori shook hands solemnly with Alexi.

"And your name, little sister?" the soldier asked.

Tanya felt suddenly shy and confused. "Oh, my name is Tanya Makarovitch." Tanya flipped her shining braids nervously over her shoulder. She saw that no one was listening.

Bravely, she plunged into her question. "I have been praying for a Bible for my Poppa, comrade, for a long time. I thought because you are a soldier . . . well, I thought perhaps you would know a place to get a Bible," she blurted.

Alexi stabbed his fists into his pockets. "Comrade soldier, you see my sister is a girl and does not understand about . . ." Alexi grew more distressed as he tried to explain.

But the soldier interrupted, "It's all right, little brother."

"But comrade," Alexi continued, glancing angrily at Tanya, "I do not think my sister has money to buy a Bible—even if you do find a place to get one."

"Why, Alexi," Tanya said, almost forgetting that the tall soldier was listening too, "I know Poppa would find a way to pay for the Bible, somehow."

Alexi glared at Tanya. Had she completely forgotten his warning about the soldiers? He wished he could tell her to keep quiet.

By now a small group of people had gathered again around Gregori. But the tall soldier did not hurry the children. He looked thoughtfully into the forest. Then in a confiding voice he bent to the children. "I don't like to disappoint you," he said, "especially this little sister who prays for a Bible." And he smiled at Tanya. "But I'm being sent away from Moscow very soon. I'm being sent to military duty in another country. I'm sorry."

Tanya forced back tears. "And the other soldiers? Are they going with you, too?" she asked.

"Yes," Gregori replied slowly, "I'm afraid, little sister, that all of us are being sent."

Then Tanya did cry. She tried not to, but she had not expected to be so disappointed. She had been sure her plan would work. "I'm sorry I bothered you, comrade soldier," she said.

"But it was not a bother," the soldier replied. And then Gregori had an idea. "Listen, when I come back to Moscow, perhaps I shall come to visit you. And perhaps," his voice brightened, "by then I shall find a Bible for us both, little sister. If I do I promise that I will deliver it to you myself!"

"Will you be gone for a long time?" Tanya tried hard to be brave but her voice choked.

"Well," the soldier admitted, "I'm afraid it will be a year or two, but I have a suggestion. Why don't you write your name in my address book? Otherwise I will not know where to bring the Bible if I do find one. You're not afraid to do that, are you?"

Tanya saw Alexi's leery expression and remembered his warning about spies, but the tall soldier was so kind. She wasn't afraid. She took the little book and pen he offered her and clearly wrote her name and address. Already she felt better.

"Thank you for talking to me, comrade soldier. May the Lord go with you," she said timidly. She turned quickly to leave before tears came again.

Gregori's friendly voice followed her. "Have faith, little sister. I think very much that God will yet answer your prayer."

Because of the exciting encounter with the soldier, it was five o'clock when the Makarovitches finally turned down the trail that branched off from the forest clearing toward the city. It seemed to Tanya that the sun had delayed especially for her so she could talk to the soldier.

As the family trudged silently through the cool woods, she thought about her conversation with Gregori. The sun sank wearily under the clouds blanketing the Western horizon. Gradually the forest darkened.

The family walked closer to Mr. Makarovitch who held the flashlight. Tanya had made Alexi promise that he wouldn't tell their parents she had asked for help in finding a Bible. But now she couldn't resist talking about the soldiers herself.

"Poppa," she said, "were you afraid at first when you went back to talk to the soldiers?" Mr. Makarovitch walked silently several steps down the path before he paused to answer.

"Well, Tanya, that is hard to say. But now it is the soldiers themselves that I am afraid for." His voice was sober. "You know it isn't going to be easy for those three soldiers. When the officials at the army base discover they are Christians, the officers will probably try to persuade the men not to follow Christ. They may ask them to spy and inform on other Christians. We must pray for those three soldiers. There may be trouble and persecution ahead for them," he said ominously.

That night when the Makarovitches were finally back in their own cozy apartment, Tanya lay awake in bed for a long time. Her mind was restless, trying to understand all that had hap-

48

pened at the meeting in the woods. Through the dark she studied the big plaque that hung on the living room wall above her head. "Bog yest lyubov—God is love."

"Dear God," Tanya prayed, "I believe You and I love You. I pray that You will help the three soldiers. I pray they will keep on loving You and following You—through everything."

The next two weeks, Tanya thought about the soldiers every night. When the Makarovitch family prayed together after the radio broadcasts, Tanya always remembered to pray for the three soldiers.

Sometimes Tanya tried to talk to Alexi about the soldiers. "I think Gregori will find us a Bible," she said to him once when they were alone.

Alexi only wrinkled his forehead and said glumly, "I hope you're right—now that you gave them our address and told them everything." His eyes reflected how troubled he was.

Sometimes Alexi wondered if he should tell his parents that Tanya had talked to the soldiers. Suspicion nagged him. "What if the soldiers were only pretending to be Christians? What if they were informers after all?"

Each day as spring skipped toward summer, the sun stayed out longer. Soon there were only three weeks of school. Then two. And both Tanya and Alexi were glad.

Finally there was only one week left. That week Tanya's delight in summer vacation was suddenly shattered.

It had happened during science class when Meria Petrovna, Tanya's teacher, was lecturing about space exploration.

"Our brave Soviet cosmonauts went thousands of miles into space," she said proudly. "Our cosmonauts looked all around the heavens, as they are called," Meria Petrovna scowled, "and they didn't see any God."

And then unexpectedly, Meria Petrovna turned to Tanya.

"Tanya," she asked, "how is it that our cosmonauts proved there is no God. Yet you, only a young girl, insist there is a God? You have told me that it is your belief in God which prevents you from joining our Young Communist Pioneers and wearing the red scarf," she accused.

"Is it true, Tanya? Do you believe there is a God?" Meria Petrovna smiled almost kindly —as if she were encouraging Tanya to give the right answer.

Respectfully, Tanya stood to answer. She felt her cheeks turn fiery. To Tanya it seemed as if the room had never been so quiet. "Dear Lord . . . help me," she prayed silently.

"Yes," Tanya said calmly, "it is true I believe in God." She felt Meria Petrovna's look of disappointment.

"I know that our cosmonauts went a long way into space," Tanya blushed, "but I'm sure that God lives in my heart. And," she struggled for words, "someday I will see God."

One student laughed. The classroom that had

been silent suddenly rippled with laughter.

Meria Petrovna sighed, "Well, Tanya Makarovitch, I wanted to give you another chance. Now I have no choice. I have given you every chance to say that you do not believe in God. But still you persist in this fanatic foolishness."

Meria Petrovna shook her head. "Since you insist you believe in God, and since you refuse to join the Young Pioneers and wear the red scarf, you also cannot come to summer camp. Summer camp is for loyal citizens, for true communists—it is not for Christians. If I let you come without your red scarf, Tanya, I will only get myself in trouble. I am sorry. I am sorry you will not change your mind."

Tanya stumbled into her seat. Tears stung her eyes, but she held them back. Everyone was staring at her—whispering and giggling. Crying would only make her humiliation worse.

Tanya was glad that science was the last class of the day. When the final bell rang, she avoided Meria Petrovna. Once outside the school gate, she ran quickly for the bus. She didn't even want to wait for Alexi.

Tanya groped up the dark cement stairs to the apartment. Her book bag weighed a ton on her shoulder. Tanya was so lost in her own despair that she didn't see her grumpy neighbor, Mrs. Gornuk, bustling down the hall. She bumped into Mrs. Gornuk's shopping bag which bulged with carrots. "Tanya Makarovitch," Mrs. Gornuk snapped, "lift your head. Look where you're going!"

Finally Tanya reached the familiar door of her own apartment. She hoped her mother would be home.

Mrs. Makarovitch sat at the table cutting cabbage for supper. She saw Tanya's drooping face and hugged her daughter.

"Did something happen at school, Tanyatchka?" she asked gently.

And then Tanya told her mother the whole story about Meria Petrovna, about the red scarf, and how everybody had laughed. "And," Tanya sobbed, "Meria Petrovna said I can't go to summer camp, Momma, because I don't belong to the Young Pioneers—because I'm the only one in our whole room who doesn't wear the red scarf."

Mrs. Makarovitch stroked Tanya's soft hair. Her hands were rough and pricked with needle marks from her work at the sewing factory. Through her tears Tanya thought of her mother. She had never heard her complain about her hard work at the factory.

"Remember, Tanyatchka," Mrs. Makarovitch comforted. "The Lord saw everything that happened today. I think He would have been proud of you."

That evening after the radio broadcast, the whole family lingered around the table and talked about Tanya's experience at school. "It's not easy," Mr. Makarovitch sympathized. "But do not forget, God has a plan for your life even in this experience. God has not forgotten you."

"And you know, Tanyatchka," Mr. Makarovitch grinned, "I think I can help you discover what God's plan is for you—at least this summer." Mr. Makarovitch looked at his wife. "Should I tell them, Galya, about the secret?"

"Secret!" Alexi leaped from the table, upsetting a vase of flowers. "Poppa, tell us!"

"It's something you've always wanted to do," Mr. Makarovitch teased.

# 5

# How Poppa's Bible Was Lost

"We're going on a trip," Mr. Makarovitch said. "We're going to Prague to see Baba."

Mrs. Makarovitch smiled joyfully. "It's true, children. Your wonderful Poppa got permission for a passport for us to go to Czechoslovakia." Mrs. Makarovitch was as excited as the children. "For ten years I haven't seen my mother—your grandmother. When she hears that you children are coming," Mrs. Makarovitch said, hugging Tanya, "Baba will bake blintzes and peroghe for a month."

Three weeks later the Makarovitches stood on the platform of the Novgorod train station. Alexi clutched the train tickets importantly.

Mr. Makarovitch carried two big suitcases and Mrs. Makarovitch held a huge box of tea wrapped in a colorful scarf. "A gift for Baba," Mrs. Makarovitch told the children proudly. "Nobody makes tea like our Russian tea!"

Tanya was responsible for a big sack filled with cheese and bread to eat on the train. She shifted the sack from hand to hand while she studied the long line of people waiting to board the train. "Were all these people going to Czechoslovakia too?" she wondered. But then she remembered. Her father had said that the train also stopped in Poland. Tanya savored the strange names—Poland, Czechoslovakia, Prague. She had never been outside the Soviet Union before.

One old woman shoved a heavy suitcase inch by inch to the train along the concrete platform. A little boy in a blue sailor cap hugged a furry bear with both hands and almost stumbled climbing onto the train.

Alexi wiggled in every direction trying to see everything at once. Suddenly he froze.

"Poppa!" He grabbed his father's arm and pointed wildly to the other side of the platform. "That man! Look! I think he's the soldier who was at the meeting—the tall soldier."

Tanya tried to see where Alexi was pointing. She poked her head through the lines of people separating her from the other side of the platform.

"Oh, Poppa, can we go find him?" she begged.

"Ivan, we better not move out of the line.

We'll miss the train and lose our places," Mrs. Makarovitch worried.

"You and the children stay here and hold our places in line. I'll hurry over and try to find the soldiers." Mr. Makarovitch turned hastily to his wife. He dropped the two suitcases in front of Alexi.

"Don't worry," he yelled back when Mr. Makarovitch was already some distance across the platform. "I'll watch the line. We won't miss the train."

Tanya wished she could have scrambled after her father, but she knew she must obey him and stay in the line. She strained to see above the crowd on the platform. "Oh, Alexi, do you really think it was comrade Gregori? Did he have a suitcase?" She jumped up to see and almost dropped the lunch sack. "Wouldn't it be wonderful if he was going to Czechoslovakia on our train? We could see him again!" she exclaimed.

Alexi lowered his voice so their mother couldn't hear. "Hah! You really are a girl," he muttered. "Listen, Tanya, maybe you should be scared. Did you ever think of that? For all you know that soldier found out we're going on a trip. Maybe he's come down to the station to follow us. You know you can't trust a soldier," Alexi scowled. "You should never have given him our address."

Tanya frowned. Why did Alexi have to be so suspicious? "I trust the soldier. Poppa trusts the soldier. You're wrong, Alexi. Those soldiers are our friends," she said with conviction and then jumped as high as she could to see if the soldier really was Gregori.

Finally Tanya located her father in the distance. He was talking to a soldier. And she was certain it was comrade Gregori. Tanya could barely stop herself from running across the platform. Mrs. Makarovitch glanced nervously at her watch, "I wonder which train the soldier is taking."

"Poppa, was it comrade Gregori? Where is he going?" Tanya shouted above the noise of the crowd and trains to her father as he hurried back. Mr. Makarovitch grabbed a suitcase and rushed toward the train steps.

"Patience, Tanyatchka. Wait until we are on the train and I'll tell you everything."

Once the family was settled inside the train compartment Mr. Makarovitch said, "It was Gregori." Since there were no other passengers in their compartment, Mr. Makarovitch spoke freely. "It is an amazing coincidence. Gregori is also traveling to Czechoslovakia."

Alexi looked alarmed, but Tanya was ecstatic. "Oh, Poppa," Tanya said, moving closer to her father, "is he on our train? Can we find him and talk to him right away?"

"No," Mr. Makarovitch replied. "He's traveling on a special military train because he is going to Czechoslovakia to work as a Russian advisor at the border."

"Well, if he's going to Czechoslovakia, maybe we can see him there," Tanya persisted.

Mr. Makarovitch smiled at his daughter's enthusiasm. "I did give him Baba's address in Prague, Tanyatchka, and I invited him to come see us if he could. But I am afraid it is not likely," he warned.

Tanya was disappointed.

"But don't look so sad," Mr. Makarovitch smiled. "The soldier hasn't forgotten you. He said to say hello to little sister and then he said he hoped you were still praying."

"That was a strange remark," Mrs. Makarovitch mused aloud.

The train lunged to a start and creaked down the tracks out of the station.

"I know why the soldier said that, Poppa," Alexi suddenly blurted. "Tanya didn't tell you. At the church meeting in the woods . . . when Tanya told you she was going to talk to Natasha . . . she went to the soldier and asked him to help her find a Bible."

"Is this true, Tanya?" Mr. Makarovitch was surprised.

Tanya felt Alexi had betrayed her. "Yes, Poppa—only Alexi shouldn't have told you. But, Poppa," she turned imploringly to her father, "the soldier said he would help me. He was very kind. I wanted it for you, Poppa," Tanya said softly.

Mrs. Makarovitch was upset. "You asked that soldier for a Bible? I'm surprised at you, Tanya. Bibles are so precious. You do not ask another Christian to find you one. If he did find one he would have a friend at church or in the army to give an extra Bible to."

"I do not want you to ask anyone again for a Bible," Mr. Makarovitch said sternly. "I know, Tanyatchka, that you meant well, but you must remember that a Bible is a treasure. Every Christian man in Leningrad wishes he could own one."

"I'm sorry, Poppa," Tanya's braids hung limp over her blue canvas coat. She had hurt her parents. "I just wanted you to have a Bible, Poppa." She sniffed back tears.

All day the train lurched and rattled through open fields and clumps of fresh green forests. In the fields, farmers were discing with bright red tractors. Once Tanya thought she spotted a bird's nest in a birch tree.

She pressed her nose against the windowpane and watched the landscape parade by. She thought about Gregori . . . about the Bible. "Poppa, did you ever have a Bible?" Tanya asked. "I mean when you were a boy?"

The train lurched forward almost toppling the lunch sack which Tanya had laid beside her on the seat. Mr. Makarovitch leaned back on the wooden train seat.

"Yes," he said, staring at the countryside blurring past the train window, "there was a time when my father had a Bible. That was long ago. We lived in a cabin on the edge of Leningrad. My father worked in a factory. Those were hard days. Stalin was our leader. Every week people disappeared.

"The police usually came during the night. They accused a citizen of crimes against the state and the citizen just disappeared—usually to prison or a work camp in Siberia. Every night we waited for a knock on the door. I remember going to bed, afraid my father would be next.

"Still," Mr. Makarovitch continued, "we were happy in those days. God gave us strength. You see, children," he explained, "we had a Bible.

"My grandfather had given the Bible to my father. It was our family's greatest treasure. My father kept it hidden in a trunk in the corner of our cabin. Every night our whole family gathered around the lantern and my father read from that special Book.

"But then 1941 came and World War II." Lines appeared in Mr. Makarovitch's face as he relived the war in his memory.

"Strashno, strashno, it was terrible," he murmured. "You have seen the monuments and you have studied about the war in school, but never could you understand until you had lived through it." Mr. Makarovitch turned with feeling to his children, "I pray God that you will never have to.

"The German soldiers invaded Russia. They reached Leningrad by the end of summer. Shells fell in the street. By fall the German soldiers had blockaded the city. We couldn't get out of the city to get food supplies. That winter was the coldest in fourteen years. I will never forget. We were starving and freezing. At the same time our city was being bombed every day.

"On Christmas day my dyadya—that would be

your great-grandfather—died. He was 85 years old and couldn't stand the hunger and cold any longer.

"Day after day the siege continued. My little sister, Olga, got sick. There was no medicine for her. The government had to give all the medicine to the wounded soldiers. There wasn't even enough food to nurse her back to health. That summer she died. We buried her with others in a mass grave. Everywhere people were dying."

Painfully Mr. Makarovitch continued his story. "Somehow my father and mother, your Uncle Vladimir, and I lived through the next year. People were so hungry they fought over a piece of bread. They ate glue and paste from paper on the walls. Some cooked dogs and rats.

"Then in 1943, two years after the siege had started, my family lost everything. We were just getting ready for bed. We heard bomber planes dive overhead. We were afraid, but by now we were almost used to them.

"There was an explosion. Suddenly our house shook. My father grabbed my brother and me and lunged through the door. Mother grabbed the samovar teapot from the table and I heard her scream, 'The Bible, the Bible, we'll lose our Bible!' She turned back to the trunk to save the Bible, but my father pulled her quickly back —a few seconds before the house exploded. All my life I will remember.

"Flames leaped to the sky and in minutes fire demolished the little log cabin that was our home." Mr. Makarovitch hesitated as agonizing memories clouded his eyes. "Well, children, you know the rest of the story. The siege lasted for 900 days. By God's mercy, somehow the rest of our family survived, but our Bible was lost —forever destroyed in the burning house."

Tanya wanted to cry. Alexi said nothing but looked grimly at the floor of the swaying train.

"Children," Mrs. Makarovitch said softly, "it is already supper time. We are alone in the compartment. Let's thank God that we have food. Let's also pray about our great hunger for a Bible."

The family joined hands and over the rumble of the train wheels, Mr. Makarovitch prayed, "Our dear God and Heavenly Father, if it be your will—we pray that some day again we might hold your Holy Book, the Bible, once more in our hands."

While the Makarovitches were praying on the train speeding them toward Czechoslovakia, two other Christians in another part of Europe were also praying—and planning a trip to Czechoslovakia.


Len and Karen Stearns, two missionaries living in Switzerland, piled their car with suitcases. The phone rang and Karen dashed inside the neat, white Swiss cottage to answer.

Breathlessly Karen returned to the car. "Oh, Len, that was the post office. They said the boxes arrived from England. Praise the Lord!

That means we have our last shipment of Russian Bibles."

"The Lord timed it just right," Len said, effortlessly lifting another heavy box into the car. "That means for sure we should start for Czechoslovakia this morning."

"Now that we're really going, Len, I'm so excited," Karen said as she added Bibles to a suitcase nearly filled with clothes. "Every time we prepare for a trip to deliver Bibles, I think of the people in Russia who want them so desperately. I guess you'll think I'm silly," she smiled. "But I find myself packing the Bible and imagining the person who will finally receive it.

"But, you know," Karen's hand rested on top of the suitcase, "every time we go, Len, I also start thinking about what's going to happen when we drive up to that border with our load of Bibles. I can't deny it. Sometimes I'm afraid to go."

Len smiled at his wife and thought how young and pretty she looked. Her long, blond hair was tied back with a red-checked ribbon. "You know," Len said, taking his wife's hand in his own, "I feel the same as you. If it were just you and I going on this trip, I'd be afraid. But God is going with us."

"And that," Karen agreed with her tall, strong husband, "makes all the difference."

Yellow sunflowers dotted the towering Swiss Alps and the mountain air was full of spring. As they drove along the steep, winding mountain pass Karen rolled down the car window to breathe in the scenic beauty.

The car sputtered and almost stopped as it crawled around a high bend in the road. "Do you think the car is going to make it?" Karen worried aloud. "Maybe our load of Bibles," Karen lowered her voice, "is too heavy for these high mountain roads."

"You're whispering!" Len laughed. "We don't have to be quiet about the Bibles yet. We're still in Switzerland!"

Karen laughed, too. "I know. I guess I'm just getting in practice.

"I love this trip through the mountains but sometimes," Karen said wistfully, "I wish we could drive straight to Russia with the Bibles and give the Bibles to the Christians ourselves."

"But, of course, that way," Len reminded, "would mean we probably would never be allowed across the border into Russia. We can be thankful the satellite countries around Russia aren't so strict about Bibles."

"But they are strict enough if they find Bibles," Karen added grimly.

"But this is still the best way," Len said. "If we can just get the Bibles safely into Czechoslovakia, you can be sure the Christians there will take them on into Russia."

"Do you realize we have 200 Bibles this time?" Karen said. "That's a lot of Bibles for the border guards not to see. But we have asked the Lord to keep us and the Bibles safe. Now all we have to do is keep praising Him."

"Yes, and keep driving," Len grinned.

By three o'clock the next afternoon, Len and Karen approached the Czechoslovakian border. They followed the highway through a grove of trees and out onto an open plain. The border spread suddenly before them . . . long rows of high barbed wire fences . . . grim guard towers. At the checkpoint gate itself a communist guard with a rifle stood at attention. Karen strained to see what was happening to the car at the front of the line.

"Len," she gasped, "they're searching everything. What's going to happen to us?"

# 6

# Facing
# the Border Guards

The Charles Bridge was suspended majestically in the early morning mist. "Tanya! Alexi!" Mrs. Makarovitch roused the sleeping children. "We're in Prague. The train will be stopping soon."

A drowsy customs officer glanced at their suitcases and parcels and waved them past the inspection. The Makarovitches crowded into the back seat of a taxi which had been waiting for passengers beside the curb. Mr. Makarovitch stacked the suitcases on the front seat with the driver. Tanya rubbed sleep from her eyes. Alexi sat straight and alert scanning every street sign, but he couldn't understand the

strange Czechoslovakian words.

The taxi sped past rows of concrete apartment buildings along the nearly deserted boulevard. It was 6 a.m. and too early for morning traffic, but long orange and yellow buses lumbered down the main avenue of Prague. The taxi driver turned abruptly off the main avenue onto a cobblestone street, and almost collided with a horse pulling a wagon full of flowers and vegetables on its way to the public market.

"Look, there's Zivikov Street!" Mrs. Makarovitch discovered a small street sign at the corner. "This is mother's street. It will only be a few minutes now."

The taxi whined to a halt in front of a tall, yellow apartment building. Cheerful red flowers bloomed in the window boxes nailed on the peeling, yellow boards.

A smiling, plump woman in a long, black dress leaned out a second-floor window. Her gray hair was piled high on her head under a net. Tanya shoved inside the apartment door. "Baba," she cried, and threw herself into her grandmother's warm arms. "Oh, Baba, I'm so glad to see you. I thought we would never get to Prague."

Baba laughed, cried, and hugged everyone all at once. "Thanks and praises to God that you have come safely so far," she said as she led the way into her small, tidy apartment. "Alexi, my own grandson. Come and sit beside me. You look just like your father! Tanya, often I have wished I could see you. Come sit here. Just let me look at you all."

"Oh, Momma," Mrs. Makarovitch cried softly and hugged Baba again. "When you left Russia to live in Czechoslovakia I thought we might never see you again. To think we are really here. To think we are in Prague. God is good!"

Tanya forgot how tired she was from the all-night trip on the train. She scurried to explore Baba's apartment. There were four rooms with high ceilings. The apartment was old but Baba had scrubbed everything—even the floors shone. Baba's windowsills were like a garden. Containers of all shapes held intriguing plants and flowers. One plant in a pot on the floor with funny green leaves grew almost to the top of the window.

Tanya spied a platter of blintzes on Baba's table. The aroma of the delicious, sweet cheese pancakes filled the room. Alexi investigated the oven and discovered that Baba had more trays of the pancakes inside. "Wow, I'm hungry, Baba!"

The Makarovitches sat for a long time around Baba's table eating blintzes, spicy sausages, drinking tea, and just talking. "Alexi, you've eaten so many blintzes, I think you are going to turn into one," Baba laughed merrily, filling the platter again with the delicious pancakes.

When the dishes were cleared from the table, Baba smoothed Tanya's silky, black braids with her wrinkled hand. "Well, children," she said, "have you thought about what you want to see in Prague? There's the old, old Karlstein Castle.

There are boat rides on the Vltava River, and of course, there's the old town square with the huge clock. When the hour strikes, little wood carved figures come out and dance in the tower."

Everyone answered at once. Mrs. Makarovitch wanted to visit the outdoor market and shop for a tablecloth to take back to Russia. Alexi had heard about the castle. "Do they really have the swords the knights fought with, Baba?" he asked excitedly.

"How is the fishing in the Vltava River?" Mr. Makarovitch wondered.

"Poppa, don't forget," Tanya whispered, "we have to look for a Bible while we're here!"

"A Russian Bible!" Baba overheard Tanya's words. Her merry eyes turned somber. "Ivan, can it be," she said sadly, "that you are still looking for a Bible? In all this time you have not been able to find one to buy in Russia?"

"We didn't want to worry you, Mother," Mrs. Makarovitch turned to Baba. "That's why I haven't told you in letters. Besides, if I had written a letter to you that we couldn't find a Bible, the censor who checks the mail might have thought we were complaining."

Baba stared warily out the window to the winding, narrow street below. She pulled the lacy curtains shut and switched on the radio. "So no one will hear us while we talk," she explained quietly.

"So things have not changed since I left Russia. For so long our Russian people have not had Bibles." With a weary sigh Baba plugged in the samovar to make tea.

"I know Christians in our church here in Prague who are trying to help take Russian Bibles into the Soviet Union." Baba settled herself in the rocking chair. "Some of these Czechoslovakian Christians travel to Western Europe when they can get a passport. They bring back Russian Bibles to Czechoslovakia and then take them on into the Soviet Union.

"But the last few months," Baba continued, "the Czechoslovakian Christians say it is very difficult even to find any Russian Bibles. There was a notice in our paper that the Russian government has ordered the leaders of Czechoslovakia to stop all Russian Bibles at the border. There is no law against bringing in Bibles, but the Russian government is afraid of the Bible."

Baba spoke softly almost as if she were afraid someone might be listening. "But I have heard there are brave Christians in the West who are still trying to bring Russian Bibles into Czechoslovakia.

"Three months ago," Baba explained, "there was a Christian from Sweden who brought several hundred Russian Bibles here to Prague. Some of my friends invited the missionary to their house for tea. I was invited also. The missionary had a very unusual experience at the border."

The Makarovitch family listened intently. Baba continued her story. "When the missionary drove up to the Czechoslovakian border, the guards were thoroughly searching the car ahead of him. The missionary knew that it was his turn next. The Russian Bibles he carried in his car were not hidden. The missionary knew the guards would discover them if they looked very hard. The missionary prayed that somehow the guards might not see the Bibles.

"At that moment, dark, threatening clouds billowed up in the sky. Rain began to pour. The guards didn't want to get wet, so they scurried inside the border station. They shouted out the station door to the missionary. 'You can go on through. There's no use getting wet.'

"So you see," Baba finished her story, "the Lord sent that rainstorm so the missionary could bring the Russian Bibles safely into our country. It was truly a miracle."

"What happened to the Bibles, Baba?" Tanya's eyes sparkled. "Do you think we could ask someone for one of those Bibles the missionary brought?"

"My dear little Tanyatchka," Baba hugged her granddaughter. "You are so young and eager. At that time I didn't know you were coming to visit. I didn't know your father had still not been able to find a Bible. So you see," she said apologetically, "I didn't ask if I could buy one of the Bibles. All the Bibles were taken the very next day to a border town outside of Prague. By now they would have all been taken into Russia."

"Don't be disappointed, Tanya," Mr. Makarovitch consoled. "Instead we must praise God that at least that many Bibles went into Russia.

Those Bibles will make some Russian Christians very, very happy."

"But, Poppa, what about us?" Tanya complained. "Do you think the Lord will ever send our family a Bible?"


Karen and Len studied the forbidding barricades ahead as they waited anxiously at the Czechoslovakian border. The long line of cars ahead reminded Karen of a snake slithering through the grass.

The cars crawled toward the guard station checkpoint—the only opening in the wall of barbed-wire fences and guard towers. Karen trembled as she watched the soldier in the small black guard tower pace back and forth, gun in hand.

Apprehensively, she glanced at the Bibles in the back of the car. "Len, do you think the guards will open our suitcases? I've tossed our coats and blankets over them, but they still look like an awful lot of suitcases for two people."

Len pondered his wife's question while he kept a close watch on the cars ahead. "You know it's possible the border guards might not even ask us to open our suitcases. They may wave us through. That's happened before. Of course, if they do open the suitcases, they will probably find the Bibles."

"And that can mean almost anything," Karen whispered. "They could lock up the Bibles and send us back to Switzerland. Of course, they might lock up the Bibles and us too."

"With instructions never to try to enter Czechoslovakia again," Len added soberly. "But, Karen, let's just trust the Lord. These are His Bibles and you and I are His too. We are not breaking any law. We are just trying to help God's people. While we're waiting, let's just praise God for bringing us here and giving us the privilege of taking these Bibles to Christians who want them so badly." Karen and Len bowed their heads and prayed.

Slowly Karen opened her eyes. The guards were now searching the second car. "We've been here 30 minutes and they spent all that time just searching one car," Karen groaned. She counted the cars ahead. "Four of them!" she exclaimed. "At this rate, we'll be here for hours yet. I don't know if I can stand the suspense."

"At least it will give us more time to pray before we actually reach the checkpoint," Len smiled reassuringly at his wife.

While Karen and Len waited, they prayed. They thought back to last fall when they had taken 300 Russian Bibles into Hungary. Karen remembered how tense she had felt that day as they approached the Hungarian border.

She and Len had overheard three French passengers in the car ahead arguing with the Hungarian guards. Hungarian law required the Frenchmen to register their hunting weapons, but they couldn't communicate with the guards who spoke only Hungarian and English. Frantically, the guards waved their arms. The three

French tourists angrily complained about the delay.

Karen remembered how Len had stepped out of their car. "Wait, here," he had told Karen. And then Len courteously offered to translate for the Hungarian guards and the three Frenchmen.

"Wow, was I ever glad that day that you could speak both French and English," Karen chuckled.

Len had translated for the guard and the French tourists. The Hungarian guard was so grateful for Len's help that he had just waved Len and Karen and their carload of 300 Bibles across the border. He had not even opened the car door.

"Wouldn't it be wonderful if that happened today?" Karen whispered to Len as their car edged closer to the Czechoslovakian border.

Finally there was only one car ahead of them. Karen watched the Czechoslovakian guard in a drab gray uniform question the driver. "I wonder what he's asking," Karen thought apprehensively.

The guard investigated every inch of the car. He ordered all the passengers out of the car and examined every piece of luggage. He lifted up the car seats and ran his hand along the frames. He even crawled under the car with a flashlight. Satisfied with his thorough search, the guard finally waved the car through.

It was their turn. Karen felt weak. "Please, Lord, we commit ourselves and our load of

Bibles to you," she prayed softly. She felt Len's quick reassuring touch on her arm.

"You will show your passports, please." The guard leaned in the car window and spoke with difficulty in English. Len held out the passport.

"You're from Switzerland? Tourists?" the guard asked frowning.

"Yes," Len smiled. "We're tourists. We're on our way to Prague. My wife has never seen Prague and we hope to spend at least a week's holiday there. We're looking forward to seeing your beautiful country. We'd like to take a boat ride on the Vltava River . . ."

But the guard interrupted Len curtly. "Step out of the car, both of you, please."

"You have suitcases in the trunk of the car?" the guard grunted. Len nodded. "Yes? All right, get them out. Let's have a look."

Karen prayed as the unsmiling guard roughly jerked the suitcases to the ground. He quickly opened one suitcase and began to lift the clothing. Angrily he pulled out a Bible.

"What's this?" he snapped.

"Bibles," Len replied calmly. "They're Russian Bibles. We're taking them as gifts for Russian Christians."

The guard was startled. "Are all these suitcases full of Bibles?" he asked gruffly.

"Not all of them. But we have brought several Bible gifts," Len replied truthfully.

"Our Czechoslovakian government," the chief guard said sternly, "cooperates fully with our comrades in the Soviet Union. Russian Bibles are not welcome in the progressive, scientific Soviet Union. They are not welcome in our country either. It is not good for Russians to be reading this book. Come with me. I will have to lock up these books and question you further."

The guard led the way into the gloomy station. He called two assistants to carry the other suitcases. "Dump those Bibles on the table," he barked at the two assistants who hastily emptied the Bibles from the suitcases and laid them out on the table.

"Bibles, Bibles," the chief guard shouted and pounded his fist angrily on the table. "What makes you think you can bring all these religious books into our country? We're atheists. We don't believe in God. We don't want these books." He snatched a Bible and slammed it to the table.

Then with a menacing smile he turned to Len and Karen who waited on the other side of the room. "I have several alternatives." His voice was hard and cruel. "I can prevent you from entering Czechoslovakia. I can see to it you never again travel in any Soviet country. Or," he sneered, "I can put you in prison. I'm not sure which alternative I should choose."

He stopped pacing around the table and thought for a moment. Suddenly, he called one of the assistant guards back into the room. "Franciuk," he commanded, "go ask our supervisor to come into the interrogation room. He'll know what we should do with our Bible-carrying tourists."

As the assistant scurried out the door, the chief guard paced around the room. He glared at Karen and Len from across the room.

Karen whispered rapidly to Len, "What will happen? Will they let us stay together? Oh, Len . . .?" Her voice was lost in a gulp of fear.

"I don't know," Len whispered quickly. "Keep praying, Karen."

Then through the window, Len spotted the supervisor—a tall soldier with red stars on his officer's hat. "Karen," Len's voice was tight, "the supervisor is a Russian soldier."

# 7

# The Miracle
# at Karlstein Castle

Tanya settled close to her grandmother on a bench in Prague's town square. "I wish Thursday would never come, Baba," Tanya said morosely.

Baba squeezed her granddaughter's hand. "Sweet little Tanyatchka, of course Thursday must come. I will be lonely when you leave," Baba admitted. "But I know you must go sometime."

Mrs. Makarovitch joined Tanya and Baba in time to overhear the conversation. "And Poppa and I must be back on our jobs by Monday," she added with a sigh. "Soon you and Alexi will be back in school, Tanyatchka."

Tanya dreaded to think about school, but she knew her mother was right. All too soon it would be time to return. Tanya tried to be hopeful. Maybe this time it would be different. Maybe her new teacher wouldn't try to force her to join the Young Communist Pioneer Club.

Lost in her reverie, Tanya wandered from the bench in a tiny park in the center of the square where she studied the towering statue of John Huss. She thought of Baba's proud explanation when they had visited the memorial statue a few days ago. "John Huss was a Christian reformer. For his convictions he was burned at the stake."

The family walked toward the bus stop from the town square. It was only three in the afternoon, but already the streets were crowded with workers from the factories who had started work at five in the morning.

The tantalizing aroma of warm apple strudel wafted from the door of a gaily decorated pastry shop. Baba opened a small black coin purse and handed some money to Alexi. "Here, Alexi," she smiled, "buy five—one for each of us for supper. Tanya, put them in here," and she handed Tanya her cloth shopping bag.

They had almost reached the bus stop when Alexi tugged on his father's sleeve. "Poppa, we can go to the Karlstein Castle tomorrow, can't we? It will be our last chance before we go home," he said eagerly.

"But I want to go boating one more time on the Vltava River," Tanya objected. "We have to go tomorrow, Poppa," she urged. "It will be our last chance. You promised we could." She grabbed hold of her father's strong hand.

"But, Poppa, just one more time to the castle," Alexi tried doggedly.

"Children, children, you are going to tear your father apart pulling his arms," Mrs. Makarovitch interrupted.

"Well," Mr. Makarovitch said tentatively, "I did promise Tanya. I said you could go boating and I do think it might be a sunny day tomorrow. But on second thought, perhaps it would be more fun to go to the castle again."

"No, Poppa, boating. That would be a lot more fun," Tanya exclaimed triumphantly.

"Well, I did give my word," Mr. Makarovitch conceded.

That night after everyone had gone to bed, Tanya lay awake. She thought about the white lace scarf Alexi had bought for her at the town square gift shop. She knew he had spent the money which he had been saving to buy a hockey stick.

The noisy cuckoo in the hall struck ten and startled Tanya to action. She crawled out of her folding bed and went to where Alexi slept on the floor. Baba had made a cozy bed from fluffy quilts. She shook her brother's shoulder. "Alexi, wake up," she whispered.

He rubbed his eyes and muttered in a disgruntled voice, "What . . . what, Tanya, I'm sleeping. Tell me tomorrow," and he turned on his pillow.

"Wait, Alexi, wait," Tanya coaxed. "I—I've

been thinking about the boat ride tomorrow."

"What about it?" Alexi mumbled.

"It was selfish of me," she hesitated, "to say I didn't want to go to the castle. I'm sorry, Alexi. Let's go to the castle tomorrow."

"You mean it?" Alexi almost leaped from under the heavy quilt.

"Sh-sh-sh. You'll wake Momma and Poppa and Baba. Of course I mean it."

"Boy, I can hardly wait for tomorrow. Poppa will be surprised," and Alexi curled contentedly in his cozy blanket.

Alexi hadn't said thank you, but Tanya knew he was pleased and she was surprised how happy she felt herself.

Karen and Len watched tensely as the Russian soldier entered the guard station. "So he's the one who is going to decide what to do with us," Karen thought. She lifted her eyes to the soldier's and expected them to be as steely cold as his harsh uniform. But they were strangely serene.

The infuriated Czechoslovakian guard who had marched Karen and Len into the guardhouse snapped to attention when the Russian soldier entered the room.

With a look of importance he pointed accusingly at the two missionaries. "Comrade, these two so-called tourists," he said to the Russian soldier, "deliberately tried to smuggle 200 anti-Soviet books into Czechoslovakia. They have tried to poison the minds of Soviet citizens."

Then the Czechoslovakian guard shook his fist at Karen and Len. "You two will see that it is unfortunate to try to trick the Czechoslovakian government and the Soviet Union."

"Oh, Len," Karen whispered. "Do you think they will let us stay together?" Len reached for his wife's hand.

The Czechoslovakian turned gravely to the Russian soldier. "You are our advisor. What do you suggest that we do, comrade, with these troublemakers?" His harsh words hung heavy in the air.

So far the Russian soldier hadn't said a word. While the Czechoslovakian guard shouted, he stood silently analyzing the situation. Karen felt his eyes upon her and Len.

When the Russian soldier spoke, there was quiet authority in his voice. He addressed the guard, "Excuse me, comrade, but there is something I don't understand. You intend to arrest these people?"

"Yes, comrade," the Czechoslovakian guard snapped decisively as if he were sure his reply would please the Russian soldier. "Would you tell me the charge, please?" the Russian soldier asked in the same even voice.

The Czechoslovakian guard grew defensive. "Well, comrade," he hedged, "you do agree they should be arrested, don't you? Perhaps I should have consulted you sooner, comrade," he said uneasily. "I certainly didn't mean to take matters into my own hands."

"I'm curious to know the charge against the two tourists. That is all," the soldier reminded the distracted Czechoslovakian guard.

"Ah, yes, the charge," the Czechoslovakian guard cleared his throat again. A sneer spread across his face as he turned maliciously toward Karen and Len. "These two so-called tourists were attempting to bring traitorous books into our country and here is the evidence." The Czechoslovakian guard gestured triumphantly to the little table in the corner of the room which was stacked with Bibles.

"And what kind of traitorous books did the tourists bring?" the Russian soldier asked.

"Bibles," the Czechoslovakian guard said in a tone that indicated the evidence was final.

A strange expression flickered across the Russian soldier's face, but he said nothing. He walked calmly to the table, picked up one of the Bibles and opened the cover. Then he turned the pages of the Bible. He examined the Bible for a long time before he placed it carefully back on the table.

"But these are not Czechoslovakian Bibles. They are Russian Bibles," the soldier's voice was taut and controlled.

"Ah, yes, I guess I forgot to mention that fact," the Czechoslovakian guard said hastily. "Of course, the fact that they are Russian only makes the offense worse. Don't you agree?"

What is the code of law which prohibits Russian Bibles from being taken across the Czechoslovakian border?" the soldier asked quietly.

"Well, of course, comrade, there is no law," the startled Czechoslovakian guard sputtered. "But our practice is . . ."

"This time I think we should abide by our actual law," the Russian soldier said tersely. "But, of course, the decision is yours. I am only here to observe."

The Czechoslovakian guard struggled to recover his stern composure in front of Karen and Len. Although she couldn't understand the conversation which was in Czechoslovakian, Karen knew the guard was flustered.

"Well," the Czechoslovakian guard stumbled uncertainly, "of course, if that is your verdict, comrade supervisor."

Then the Czechoslovakian guard turned brusquely to Karen and Len. "This is very irregular, but since our supervisor has indicated his decision, I am willing to consider that perhaps you brought these books in your ignorance— these Bibles," he glanced distastefully at the table in the corner.

"I have changed my mind," he said, suddenly generous. "I shall let you go. In fact, if you wish to see our beautiful country of Czechoslovakia, I shall even allow you to proceed past the border."

Karen wished she could run to the car and drive away before the cruel Czechoslovakian guard changed his mind. But suddenly, to her astonishment, she heard Len speak steadily and politely to the Czechoslovakian guard.

"Thank you," he said, "but I am sorry. We

are not ready to go."

"What?" the guard fumed. "I do not understand you."

Len continued firmly, "You have kept our property—the 200 Bibles. But they belong to me. Perhaps I will have to return to Switzerland with them because no one wants them here. But still you have no reason to keep them. There is no law that says I should not keep my own property."

The Czechoslovakian guard's face grew swollen and furious. He seemed almost too stunned by Len's boldness to answer. Finally he exploded to the Russian soldier, "Now, comrade soldier, what do you think of our two tourists? We try to help them and this is how they act!"

But the Russian soldier kept his same mild composure. "Come, come," he said with quiet dignity to the furious Czechoslovakian guard. "Let us not allow these tourists to disturb us, comrade. You make too much of their nonsense. What a lot of talking and argument about a stack of old books. Surely if the Bibles contain nothing but foolishness, they cannot corrupt the great Soviet people. As the tourist says, if no one wants them, then he will have the work of hauling them all the way back to Switzerland." The Russian soldier laughed heartily. "That would be a good joke on our tourists, now wouldn't it?"

At first the Czechoslovakian guard stared in disbelief at the Russian advisor. "I—I guess that would be a good joke on our tourists," he said uncertainly. "Ha—ha—ha," the Czechoslovakian guard tried to laugh, but he seemed puzzled.

Karen knew she had seen a miracle when she heard the Czechoslovakian guard say magnanimously, "All right, take your Bibles, Mr. Tourist. You will have the work of carting them home again. But don't ever try to bring any more of your corrupt literature across our border. You have wasted our time," he threatened angrily as Karen and Len walked toward the Bibles.

His expression inscrutable, the Russian soldier handed Karen and Len their passport when the Bibles were finally loaded. "You may proceed to Prague," he said.

"Oh, Lord, oh, Lord, thank You," Karen whispered as they drove safely away from the border. "Praise the Lord, the King of Heaven," she sang softly with joy in her voice. "At his feet thy tribute lay . . ."

When they were safely out of sight of the foreboding border, Len fumbled for his passport in his coat pocket. "Here, Karen, better put this back in our travel folder before we lose it."

"I wonder if the Russian soldier stamped anything inside," Karen said, curiously opening the cover. "He took it into the back room, you know."

"Oh, oh, Len!" Karen gasped. A small note fluttered out of the passport.

"Read it, Karen. Don't just look at it." Len kept his eyes on the road, but his voice was urgent.

Slowly Karen read the words aloud which

were painstakenly written in English.

"I am a Christian. Please, I would like two Bibles. I will be in Prague in three days on my day off. Please meet me at the following place."

The Russian soldier had enclosed a carefully drawn map indicating the rendezvous point in Prague.

"That's the end of the note," Karen said. "It isn't signed, but I think I know why! It is incredible, Len. Only God could have planned a miracle like this!" Karen's eyes sparkled.

"Wow," Len exclaimed. "When I think of what could have happened to us, Karen. Who would have thought the Lord would have answered our prayers by sending us a Christian border inspector? And a Russian soldier on top of it!" he exclaimed.

"Oh, Len, we can meet him in Prague, can't we, and give him his Bibles? What a beautiful experience. I'm so excited to think he was a Christian," she repeated, cherishing the wonder of it all. "Oh, Len, I can't wait until Thursday."


Tanya hadn't expected to enjoy herself so much at the castle, but the morning was filled with adventure. Since she and Alexi had been at the castle before, their parents let them climb up the hill to the castle themselves. Mrs. Makarovitch was busy packing. Baba was baking cookies to eat on the train and Mr. Makarovitch had gone to buy the train tickets back to Leningrad. "Look how foggy it is!" Tanya exclaimed, looking at the city of Prague far below them. "It's a good thing we didn't go boating after all."

Tanya watched the buses filled with tourists unloading in the courtyard. A group of Czechoslovakians dressed in colorful Bohemian costumes climbed off one bus. They eagerly snapped photos of the mammoth castle, the beautiful garden, and the stately old church— all landmarks of the ancient castle grounds.

"Come on, Tanya," Alexi called. "Let's go see the castle first." Inside the wide pillared door, a guide in a crisp blue uniform was showing tourists through the ancient castle banquet hall. She spoke in Russian and the children stopped to listen.

"This grand banquet hall is so huge that the Bohemian nobles would bring their prize horses inside the castle and present horse shows while their guests dined at the banquet tables." Alexi and Tanya trailed after the guide, absorbed in her intriguing explanations.

In the castle gardens, a Russian soldier lingered by a flower bed. Although he appeared relaxed, there was a determined intensity about his eyes. He scanned the faces of each person that passed. Suddenly he recognized the two missionaries whom he had seen at the border.

"I see you followed my map correctly," he smiled with pleasure at Len and Karen, but he spoke quietly. His voice dropped even lower, "I must not be seen talking to you. It would not be good for any of us." He walked slowly as he led them out of the castle ground to a high bluff that overlooked the city in front of the castle.

"We will stop by this wall here where there are no people," he instructed quietly. "Now while we talk, if you will just slip the two Bibles toward me along the top of the wall, I will drop them in my briefcase." The soldier stared off as if he were admiring the panorama of the city spread before him. He never glanced at his hands. He quickly slid the Bibles which Len passed along the railing into his briefcase.

"My dear brother and sister," he said, still looking away in the distance and speaking only casually to Karen and Len, "how I wish I could thank you and show my great gratitude to you openly. But I cannot even shake your hand. I must dissolve back into the crowd and go my way and you will go yours. I pray fervently for you. With all my heart I thank the Lord for what you have done." And the soldier was gone.


Tanya and Alexi had explored every room of the castle. "Let's go inside the church just once more," Tanya urged. "It's so beautiful. I love to see the candles burning by the statues."

"We can't," Alexi exclaimed, glancing at the new watch his parents had given him for his thirteenth birthday. "Do you know it's already 3:30?" He hurried toward the door.

"I hope we aren't late," Tanya worried as they squeezed through the crowd. "We promised Momma and Poppa we'd be home on time for sure."

They walked hastily through the castle garden. "I wish we could run," Alexi said impatiently. "But there are so many people we'd bump into everybody."

"Alexi," Tanya grabbed her brother's arm. "Look, coming up the path. Isn't that Gregori? It is Gregori!" she squealed and dashed ahead to meet him. She was so excited, she didn't wait to see her brother's face grow pinched and white with fear.

"It is the little sister from Leningrad!" Gregori recognized Tanya immediately. "And the little brother," he said greeting Alexi warmly.

"Oh, comrade soldier," Tanya's words tumbled out. "Poppa said you were coming to Czechoslovakia, but he said we would probably never get to see you while we are here. It is a miracle!"

Gregori smiled deeply. "It is not long I have walked in the Christian way, young brother and sister, but I am beginning to understand what a way of miracles it really is. Come, I will tell you about a miracle. But we must walk to a place where we can speak without being heard."

Gregori led the children toward the same secluded bluff in front of the castle. Tanya hurried to keep pace with Gregori's long steps. She turned impatiently to tug at Alexi who lagged behind. "Hurry!" she urged, but Alexi's strange expression startled her. She had never seen her brother so frightened before. His eyes were wide and scared. Slowly he followed Tanya and the soldier to the high bluff.

"Do you remember the last time we met? Do you remember what you asked me then?" Gregori asked Tanya when they reached the low stone wall bordering the edge of the cliff. Tanya remembered her parents' reproving words and stared embarrassed at the ground.

"Today, by a miracle, I have the answer to that prayer, little sister." Gregori unlatched his briefcase. Alexi turned as if he were ready to run.

"Look quickly!" the soldier said to the children. Tanya recognized the two black books first. Alexi carefully reached into the briefcase and ran his trembling fingers across the stiff, black covers. Slowly Alexi turned to Gregori. His eyes filled with admiration.

"Oh, comrade soldier," Tanya gasped. "Where . . . how?" she tried to ask every question at once.

"It is a long and wonderful miracle," Gregori smiled, "and I shall tell you every word. But I think I should deliver you and your new Bible home to your Momma and Poppa first."

Tanya reached for the soldier's hand. Then Gregori put his lanky arm around Alexi's shoulder. Tanya turned to her brother. His face was flushed and happy. She knew he was no longer afraid of the Russian soldier.

Tanya, the Russian soldier, and Alexi were ready for the city unfolding before them. Fog had blown away from the Vltava River and the Charles Bridge arched invitingly before. It seemed to Tanya that it might lead anywhere.

This story of "Tanya and the Border Guard" is based on true experiences which emerged from information the author gathered during extensive travels inside the Soviet Union and the communist satellite countries.

Anita Deyneka, author of "Tanya and the Border Guard," is the wife of Peter Deyneka, Jr., Assistant General Director of the Slavic Gospel Association, which sponsors 120 missionaries in 22 countries. Mr. Deyneka and many of the missionaries of this organization are of Russian heritage.

This mission is responsible for several hundred Christian radio broadcasts transmitted each month into the U.S.S.R. The Slavic Gospel Association also delivers Bibles and Christian literature into the communist countries.

SLAVIC GOSPEL ASSOCIATION, Inc.

P.O. BOX 1122

WHEATON, ILLINOIS 60187

# THE PICTURE BIBLE
## FOR ALL AGES

Do you have ALL SIX books?

**Vol. 1—CREATION: Gen. 1 to Ex. 19.** All the action from "In the beginning" to the Flight . . . in pictures!

**Vol. 2—PROMISED LAND: Ex. 20 to I Sam. 16.** Moses, Ten Commandments, wanderings, fall of Jericho.

**Vol. 3—KINGS AND PROPHETS: I Sam. 16 to I Kings 21.** Shows David and Goliath, wisdom of Solomon.

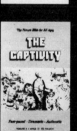

**Vol. 4—THE CAPTIVITY: I Kings 21 to Mal.** Covers the Babylonian captivity, prophecies of Jesus' coming.

**Vol. 5—JESUS: Mt. to John.** Dramatically shows the birth, teaching, miracles, final triumph of Christ.

(Cont.)